1日1分鐘新多益

# 必考單字片語背誦集

劉慧如
James Baron 編著

ESSENTIAL TOEIC VOCABULARY & PHRASES

隨身攜帶！隨時學習！

書泉出版社 印行

# Preface / 作者序

一日一分鐘多益系列叢書，承蒙五南出版社的主編及各部門幫忙，終於一路從單字、片語，到這本單字片語書，每一本都是編輯大人、我的合作作者，以及我自己用心的作品。這本書的合作作者是來自英國的紳士James Baron。他是位傑出的英語工作者，在英語寫作的領域裡有非常傲人的表現。其實，當然最要感謝的是支持我們的讀者，不吝給予回饋與指教，讓我們更有信心繼續把這個系列作得更好。

這一本是將前面兩本單字與片語的例句重新撰寫，提供讀者更多學習的資源，同時對讀

者而言也可以是一個複習的機會。接下來我們還會依序推出文法、閱讀單元；同時，第一本的單字書也即將改版囉！請讀者們期待並繼續支持。

在現今的職場上，英語已經不是一個加分的能力，而是近乎基本常識。隨著臺灣市場的國際化，競爭也隨之國際化，讓我們藉著認真準備這個國際認證且辨識度高的多益考試，全面地提升英語能力。

慧如

# Contents / 目錄

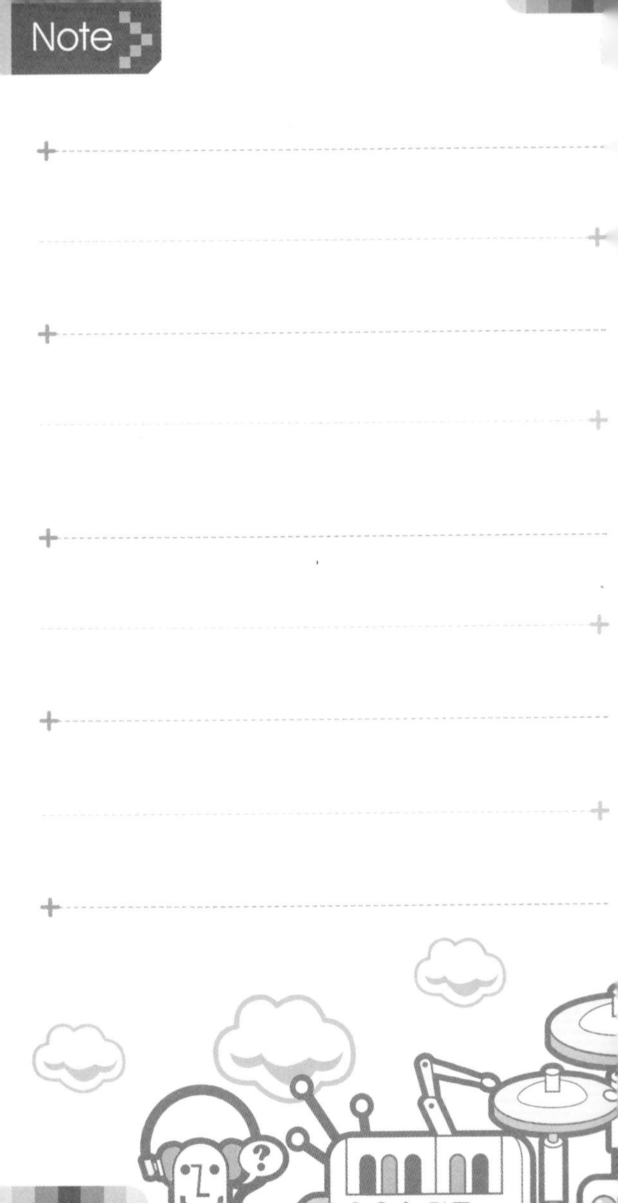
Note

# 01 / 新多益必考單字列表

Note

| | |
|---|---|
| **access**<br>['æksɛs]<br>名<br>取得 | Every time I try and log into my online account, I keep getting a message saying **access** denied.<br>每次我嘗試要登入我的網路帳號，都一直出現登入失敗的訊息。 |
| **acquisition**<br>[ˌækwə'zɪʃən]<br>名<br>收穫，取得 | Analysts found the software corporation's **acquisition** of the small startup a strange decision.<br>分析師覺得這間軟體公司取得這家新成立的小公司是個奇怪的決定。 |
| **additional**<br>[ə'dɪʃənl̩]<br>形<br>更多的；進一步的 | When you've finished filling out this form with your personal details, you can add any **additional** information in this box here.<br>你填完表格裡的個人資料後，你可以在這個欄位裡填入任何其他相關的資訊。 |

| | |
|---|---|
| **adjustable**<br>[ə'dʒʌstəbḷ]<br>形<br>可調整的 | All of the chairs on this train are **adjustable**, affording passengers maximum comfort.<br>為了要提供乘客最佳的舒適度，火車上所有的椅子都是可以調整的。 |
| **affluence**<br>['æfluəns]<br>名<br>富裕者 | Although this city is not well-developed, there are small pockets of **affluence** scattered around the suburbs.<br>雖然這個城市尚未發展成熟，不過在郊區居住著一些富裕的家庭。 |
| **allege**<br>[ə'lɛdʒ]<br>動<br>宣稱 | Corruption is rife in the government, a newspaper has **alleged** in a recent report.<br>一份報紙報導宣稱貪腐正在政府中蔓延。 |

| | |
|---|---|
| **alternative**<br>[ɔl'tɝnətɪv]<br>形<br>替代的；二擇一的 | If the restaurant you want to go to is fully booked for Saturday, do you fancy going to the one nearby as an **alternative**?<br>如果你週六想去的那間餐廳已經沒位子了，你想去那附近另一家餐廳嗎？ |
| **amendment**<br>[ə'mɛndmənt]<br>名<br>修法 | Opposition legislators say **amendments** to the bill need to be drawn up before it can be passed.<br>反對黨立法委員表示這個法案的修法必須在它被通過前先提出草案。 |
| **assume**<br>[ə'sjum]<br>動<br>認為，認定 | It is supreme arrogance to **assume** you know better than other people all the time.<br>如果你總是認為自己比其他人優越，那就太驕傲了。 |

| | |
|---|---|
| **astonishment**<br>[ə'stanɪʃmənt]<br>名<br>驚訝 | There was **astonishment** in the courtroom when the verdict was passed down.<br>當法庭裡判決出爐時，大家都很驚訝。 |
| **astronomical**<br>[ˌæstrə'namɪkl̩]<br>形<br>龐大的 | I wouldn't book a vacation with that travel agency as they charge **astronomical** fees.<br>因為那間旅行社收費太高了，我絕對不會跟他們買任何旅程。 |
| **attain**<br>[ə'ten]<br>動<br>達到；取得 | Although he was relatively young, the soldier had already **attained** a high rank in the army.<br>雖然這位士兵還算年輕，他在軍隊裡卻已經有蠻高的階級。 |

**aviation**
[ˌevɪˈeʃən]
名
航行

My friend has just completed a course in basic **aviation**, and intends to become a pilot.
我的朋友剛剛完成了初級的飛行課程，他想要當飛行員。

**backlash**
[ˈbækˌlæʃ]
名
強烈反應

Politicians need to exercise some restraint when they speak, or they could wind up facing a **backlash** from the public.
政治人物在他們說話時應該有所節制，不然他們有可能會引起大眾的強烈反彈。

**bailout**
[ˈbelˌaut]
名
紓困

Let's hope the EU **bailout** plan works, or we'll all be tightening our belts in the near future.
讓我們對於歐盟紓困案抱持希望，否則我們在未來都得要勒緊褲帶了。

| | |
|---|---|
| **barricade**<br>['bærə,ked]<br>動<br>路障；困在 | Realizing the criminal had **barricaded** himself in the house with a hostage, the police called for backup.<br>當瞭解到嫌犯把自己和人質困在屋裡，警方請求支援。 |
| **bellwether**<br>['bɛl,wɛðɚ]<br>名<br>前導者 | Developments within the corporation invariably serve as a **bellwether** for the rest of the industry.<br>公司的發展總是成為同產業的前導。 |
| **bestow**<br>[bɪ'sto]<br>動<br>贈與 | Every year, Queen Elizabeth I of the UK **bestows** honors on people who have contributed to society.<br>每一年，英國女王伊莉莎白一世都會贈勳給對社會有貢獻的人士。 |

| | |
|---|---|
| **binding**<br>['baɪndɪŋ]<br>形<br>有約束力的；綁約的 | Rather than sign a **binding** contract, the two businessmen sealed the deal with a verbal agreement.<br>這兩位生意人以口頭約定，而非簽署約束性合約，敲定了生意。 |
| **booming**<br>[bumɪŋ]<br>形<br>蓬勃的；響亮的 | Our uncle has a great, **booming** voice that often scares people.<br>我們的叔叔有著大聲、宏亮的嗓子，經常嚇到人。 |
| **brainchild**<br>['bren,tʃaɪld]<br>名<br>主意 | Some scholars argue that the telephone was actually the **brainchild** of the Italian-American Antonio Meucci, rather than Alexander Graham Bell.<br>有些學者認為電話事實上是義大利裔美國人安東尼奧木西的發明，而非亞歷山大葛拉漢貝爾的創意。 |

**brew**
[bru]
動
醞釀

I get the impression that trouble is **brewing** between those two.
我有種感覺那兩個人之間有點問題。

**butler**
['bʌtlɚ]
名
管家

In the old days, many wealthy people had **butlers**, but now it has become more of a rarity.
在以前，很多有錢的人都有管家，但現在這很少見了。

**canvass**
['kænvəs]
動
遊說

The young man braved the frosty conditions and went out **canvassing** for the local politician.
這年輕人勇於面對目前的僵局，而且出面去遊說當地的政客。

| | |
|---|---|
| **cap**<br>[kæp]<br>名<br>蓋子 | Please replace the **cap** on the bottle after you've poured yourself a drink.<br>請你在倒完水之後，把瓶蓋重新蓋上。 |
| **captivating**<br>['kæptəˌvetɪŋ]<br>形<br>令人神魂顛倒的，迷倒眾生的 | Every actor in the play was excellent, but I found the lead female's performance particularly **captivating**.<br>這齣劇裡所有演員都表現優異，不過我覺得女主角的演出尤其傑出。 |
| **catalyst**<br>['kætḷɪst]<br>名<br>催化劑 | Protests in Tunisia in late 2010 served as the **catalyst** for regime change throughout the Arab world.<br>2010年底在突尼西亞的抗爭扮演了阿拉伯世界政權改變的催化劑。 |

**cease**
[sis]
動
停止

Please **cease** prattling on – you're really annoying me!
請你不要一直說話了好嗎？你真的讓我生氣了。

**civilian**
[sɪ'vɪljən]
名
平民

Following the massacre, an international force was sent to the country to protect **civilians**.
在一個屠殺後，一個國際組織被派遣到這個國家來保護人民。

**clientele**
[ˌklaɪən'tɛl]
名
客群

The restaurant's **clientele** has always been a select bunch with very specific tastes.
這間餐廳的客群一直是一群有特別品味的精選客人。

| | |
|---|---|
| **clipboard**<br>['klɪpˌbord]<br>名<br>筆記板 | Having noticed the young woman with a **clipboard** conducting a survey, I walked the other way.<br>我注意到有個女孩手拿著筆記板做市調，就往另一個方向走了。 |
| **comfort**<br>['kʌmfɚt]<br>動<br>安慰 | My mother always **comforts** me when I'm going through a tough time.<br>每當我經歷困難時，我的母親總是會安慰我。 |
| **compound**<br>['kɑmpaund]<br>名<br>宅院 | Military hardware and top secret technology was stored in the **compound**.<br>軍方的設備和極機密的科技都存放在這個宅院。 |

| | |
|---|---|
| **compre-hensive**<br>[ˌkamprɪ'hɛn-sɪv]<br>形<br>易懂的 | Barry's fed up because his favorite football team was on the end of a **comprehensive** thrashing at the weekend.<br>拜瑞受夠了他最喜歡的足球隊在週末一直處於明顯的劣勢。 |
| **conducive**<br>[kən'djusɪv]<br>形<br>有助益的 | It goes without saying that a balanced diet and plenty of exercise are **conducive** to good health.<br>不諱言的，均衡飲食和適量的運動對健康是有助益的。 |
| **conspiracy**<br>[kən'spɪrəsɪ]<br>名<br>陰謀，密謀 | Some people still insist that there was a **conspiracy** behind the death of Princess Diana.<br>有些人還是認為黛安娜王妃的死因是個陰謀。 |

| | |
|---|---|
| **contrap-tion** [kən'træpʃən] 名 新奇的發明 | The earliest motorcars were really clumsy **contraptions**. 最初的電動車真的是笨拙的發明。 |
| **copywrit-ing** ['kɑpɪ,raɪtɪŋ] 名 廣告撰寫；文編 | Hugh isn't the most creative person in the office, but he has good basic **copywriting** skills. 休並不是辦公室裡最有創意的人，但是他有極佳的文編技巧。 |
| **counteract** [,kauntə'ækt] 動 應付；中和 | Every day I have to take a couple of pills to **counteract** the effects of this skin complaint I have. 我每天都得服用好幾顆藥來應付我的皮膚病的影響。 |

| | |
|---|---|
| **dash**<br>[dæʃ]<br>動<br>擊毀；匆忙做到 | Realizing he had just 10 minutes before the post office closed, Ernie **dashed** down the street clutching the postcard.<br>當恩尼知道郵局再十分鐘就要關門，他趕忙跑去買了明信片。 |

| | |
|---|---|
| **decelerate**<br>[di'sɛlə,ret]<br>動<br>降低速度 | **Decelerating** as quickly as possible, Matt was still unable to avoid crashing into the back of the van.<br>雖然麥特已經盡量減慢速度了，但還是無可避免的追撞上了小貨車。 |

| | |
|---|---|
| **defense**<br>[dɪ'fɛns]<br>名<br>守衛 | The champion celebrated another successful **defense** of his title.<br>這位冠軍慶祝他再次成功保住他的冠軍頭銜。 |

**degrade**
[dɪ'gred]
動
降低身分

While Jamal loved hip-hop, he couldn't deny that some of his favorite songs contained lyrics that were **degrading** to women.
雖然傑爾摩喜歡街舞，但他也無法否認某些他喜歡的歌曲的歌詞是對女性不敬的。

**demotion**
[dɪ'moʃən]
名
降職

Following the inquiry into corruption in the police force, several officers faced **demotion**.
在針對警紀腐敗的詢問之後，好幾位警員面臨降職。

**discern**
[dɪ'zɝn]
動
辨識

Is that a faint look of amusement I can **discern** on Susan's face?
我在蘇珊的臉上好像看到一抹開心的表情哦！

| | |
|---|---|
| **dismal**<br>['dɪzml̩]<br>形<br>陰暗的；負面的 | Bradley couldn't believe he had shelled out so much money to watch such a **dismal** performance by the rock group.<br>布萊德利無法置信他竟然花了這麼多錢來看這個搖滾樂團如此糟糕的演出。 |
| **dispenser**<br>[dɪ'spɛnsɚ]<br>名<br>販賣機 | To keep the customers satisfied, the fast-food restaurant added a second drinks **dispenser** on the second floor.<br>為了讓顧客滿意，這間速食餐廳在二樓又增設了一臺飲料販賣機。 |
| **diversification**<br>[daɪˌvɝsəfə'keʃən]<br>名<br>多樣化經營 | If we are to increase revenues, **diversification** will be an integral part of our strategy.<br>如果我們要創造營收，多樣化經營必將成為我們策略中不可或缺的部分。 |

**dividend**
['dɪvəˌdɛnd]
名
股息

Critics of **dividend** payouts argue that corporations would be better served reinvesting profits into R & D and expansion.
針對股利分發的評論者強調把利潤再投入研發部門和公司擴展，對企業的發展是比較好的。

**dog**
[dɔg]
動
纏，煩

I've blocked that guy on Facebook as he just won't stop **dogging** me.
因為那個人一直在臉書上煩我，我已經將他封鎖了。

**drain**
[dren]
名
下水道

Raymond struggled to retrieve his keys after he dropped them into the **drain**.
雷蒙想盡辦法把他掉在水溝的鑰匙撿起來。

| | |
|---|---|
| **dramatically**<br>[drə'mætɪkl̩ɪ]<br>副<br>戲劇化地 | Improving your fitness will **dramatically** increase your chances of success in this competition.<br>加強你的體能，一定可以很戲劇化的（大幅度的）增加你在這次比賽成功的機會。 |
| **drowsy**<br>['drauzɪ]<br>形<br>昏昏欲睡的 | Pick me up a cup of coffee on your way back from the park, would you? I'm getting really **drowsy**.<br>你可以在從公園回來的路上幫我買杯咖啡嗎？我越來越頭昏腦脹了。 |
| **dubious**<br>['djubɪəs]<br>形<br>曖昧的，含糊不清的；令人懷疑的 | I've seen the replay of that incident in the soccer match several times, and I still think it was a **dubious** decision by the referee.<br>我反覆看了幾次那場足球賽中發生的意外，我還是覺得裁判的判決令人起疑。 |

**elude**
[ɪ'lud]
動
躲避，藏匿

The criminal **eluded** capture for a month until he was finally tracked down.
這名罪犯在被找到前，藏匿了近一個月。

**emerge**
[ɪ'mɝdʒ]
動
從困境中擺脫

The press had written the presidential candidate off because of a lack of charisma, but after an impressive speech, he **emerged** as a real contender.
輿論之前對這位總統候選人缺乏領導魅力一直有負面的評論，但是在一場令人印象深刻的演說後，他躋身而為一個真正的競爭者。

**endanger**
[ɪn'dendʒɚ]
動
使危險

By driving in such a reckless fashion, the man **endangered** the lives of everyone in the car.
由於他莽撞的開車方式，這個人讓車裡其他乘客的生命備受威脅。

| | |
|---|---|
| **equivalent**<br>[ɪ'kwɪvələnt]<br>形<br>同等級的 | Give me those euros you have left over from your trip to Spain, and I will give you the **equivalent** amount in US dollars.<br>你把去西班牙玩時剩下的歐元給我，我給你等值的美金。 |
| **equivocal**<br>[ɪ'kwɪvək!]<br>形<br>模稜兩可的 | We had hoped that this research would give us a definite conclusion, but the findings are **equivocal**.<br>我們曾經希望這項研究可以給我們帶來明確的結果，但是卻得到模稜兩可的發現。 |
| **escalate**<br>['ɛskə,let]<br>動<br>擴大 | Given the rapidly **escalating** costs, I'll be amazed if this public works project is ever completed.<br>眼看著成本急速的上漲，如果這個公共工程真的完工，我將會很驚訝。 |

| | |
|---|---|
| **excursion**<br>[ɪk'skɜ·ʒən]<br>名<br>短程旅遊 | Are you going to join us on the company's annual **excursion** next month?<br>你下個月要跟我們一起去公司的年度旅遊嗎？ |
| **explosive**<br>[ɪk'splosɪv]<br>形<br>爆發性的 | The runner's **explosive** start to the race ensured he claimed the gold medal.<br>這位跑者具爆發力的起跑奠定了他的金牌之路。 |
| **extol**<br>[ɪk'stol]<br>動<br>讚揚 | Alana has been **extolling** the virtues of her new fitness regime to all her friends.<br>愛蓮娜最近一直對朋友讚揚她的新運動方式的好處。 |

| | |
|---|---|
| **extravagance** [ɪk'strævəgəns] 名 浪費；奢侈品 | When I was a student, I was so broke all the time that I couldn't afford any of the **extravagances** I enjoy now. 當我還是學生的時候，我總是很窮，所以無法負擔任何我現在喜歡的奢侈品。 |
| **faction** ['fækʃən] 名 小團體 | **Factions** within the political party are increasingly causing tensions. 這個政黨裡的小團體造成緊張的升溫。 |
| **familiarize** [fə'mɪljə͵raɪz] 動 熟悉 | Anytime I go off backpacking in a foreign country, I make it my business to **familiarize** myself with the language and customs. 每當我在國外自助旅行時，我總會盡力融入當地的語言和習俗。 |

| | |
|---|---|
| **feasible**<br>['fizəbḷ]<br>形<br>合適的；可行的 | The head of the construction team informed the local council that the plans to extend the city hall were **feasible** but that the project would be costly.<br>工程隊的主管知會市議會說市政廳要擴建是可行的，但這工程會花不少錢。 |
| **firewall**<br>['faɪrwɔl]<br>名<br>防火牆 | Facebook is inaccessible in China because of a government-enforced **firewall**.<br>臉書在大陸是無法登入的，因為政府加強了防火牆。 |
| **fluctuate**<br>['flʌktʃu,et]<br>動<br>波動 | Interest rates **fluctuated** for several months before finally stabilizing.<br>利率在最後穩定前波動了好幾個月。 |

| | |
|---|---|
| **forecast**<br>['for,kæst]<br>名<br>預測 | Don't put too much stock in the weather **forecast** for this weekend as they often get it wrong.<br>不要太相信本週末的氣象預報，因為他們經常出錯。 |
| **forecast**<br>['for,kæst]<br>動<br>預報 | Analysts **forecast** growth in the steel industry next quarter.<br>分析師預測鋼鐵工業下一季的成長率。 |
| **forum**<br>['forəm]<br>名<br>論壇 | Delegates from many nations attended the **forum** on renewable energies.<br>來自許多國家的代表都出席這次針對再生能源的論壇。 |

| | |
|---|---|
| **fundamental**<br>[ˌfʌndəˈmɛntl̩]<br>名<br>基礎概念 | My dad taught me the **fundamentals** of golf when I was a kid, so I have a pretty good idea of what I'm doing.<br>孩提時期，我的父親教導我高爾夫球的基礎，所以我現在很有概念。 |
| **gripe**<br>[graɪp]<br>動<br>發牢騷 | That old fellow next door is always **griping** about something.<br>隔壁那位老人家總是在抱怨著。 |
| **handy**<br>[ˈhændɪ]<br>形<br>方便的 | It's always **handy** to have a spare set of keys with a neighbor in case you get locked out of your house.<br>鄰居那裡放一把備用鑰匙總是比較方便的，免得你被鎖在門外。 |

| | |
|---|---|
| **heed**<br>[hid]<br>動<br>遵守 | **Heed** your mother's advice and stop hanging around with those guys.<br>聽你母親的勸告吧！別再跟那些人混在一起了。 |
| **ignite**<br>[ɪg'naɪt]<br>動<br>引起 | Tensions between the two nations were at an all-time high, and diplomats feared any little incident could **ignite** a conflict.<br>兩國間的緊張情勢達到有史以來最緊繃的狀態，雙方外交官都擔心任何一點小事件都會引起衝突。 |
| **implicate**<br>['ɪmplɪ,ket]<br>動<br>暗示 | The suspect in the murder inquiry denied any involvement in the crime, but **implicated** another man.<br>被偵訊的謀殺嫌疑犯否認牽涉犯刑，但是指涉另一個人的犯案。 |

**impose**
[ɪm'poz]
動
強加

Because she was one of the smartest and most popular girls at school, Imogen was often able to **impose** her will on her classmates.

因為她是學校裡最聰明且最受歡迎的女生之一，依茉珍通常都可以讓同學照她的話做事。

**incentive**
[ɪn'sɛntɪv]
名
動機；鼓勵

The only way to guarantee improved performances from your employees is to offer them solid **incentives**.

唯一可以保證讓你的員工表現進步的方法就是提供明確的鼓勵。

**incident**
['ɪnsədn̩t]
名
事件

Accepting his brother's apology for the misunderstanding between the two of them, Johan said he would rather forget the **incident**.

約翰接受了他哥哥針對他們兩人誤會的道歉，他說寧願忘記這個事件。

| | |
|---|---|
| **indictment**<br>[ɪn'daɪtmənt]<br>名<br>控訴 | That there is still so much poverty in our city is an **indictment** of the mayor's performance.<br>我們的都市裡還有很多貧窮問題，是對這市長政治作為的指控之一。 |
| **inevitable**<br>[ɪn'ɛvətəbl]<br>形<br>不可避免的 | After Joel came home late from the party, he prepared himself for the **inevitable** nagging from his mother.<br>喬在參加派對晚歸時就已經知道他無可避免會被母親念上一頓了。 |
| **infrastruc-ture**<br>['ɪnfrə,strʌktʃɚ]<br>名<br>基礎建設 | At the present time, the country lacks the **infrastructure** required to develop its agricultural industry.<br>目前這個階段，這個國家缺乏發展農業所需的基礎建設。 |

| | |
|---|---|
| **instrumental**<br>[ˌɪnstrə'mɛntl̩]<br>形<br>有幫助 | Praise is due to the sales team as it was their pitch that was **instrumental** in winning us this contract.<br>功勞真的是屬於業務單位的，因為他們的行銷幫助我們贏得這個合約。 |
| **intensive**<br>[ɪn'tɛnsɪv]<br>形<br>緊湊的 | Ahead of my trip to Brazil, I decided to try an **intensive** language course in Portuguese.<br>在我去巴西旅遊之前，我決定要嘗試上一堂密集的葡萄牙語課程。 |
| **intricacy**<br>['ɪntrəkəsɪ]<br>名<br>錯綜複雜 | The **intricacy** of the design on this dress is what attracted me to it.<br>這件衣服複雜的設計是它吸引我的地方。 |

| | |
|---|---|
| **languish**<br>['læŋgwɪʃ]<br>動<br>長期受苦 | We need to pull our socks up, otherwise we'll be **languishing** behind the competition at the end of the year.<br>我們必須要提振效率了，不然到了年底我們一定會因為落後我們的競爭者而欲振乏力。 |
| **legacy**<br>['lɛgəsɪ]<br>名<br>遺產；留給後人的東西 | Leaders are nearly always concerned with their **legacy** after they leave office.<br>領導者去職後，幾乎都很在意他們留下來的影響力。 |
| **liquidity**<br>[lɪkwɪdətɪ]<br>名<br>流通性資產 | The market is currently defined by a high degree of **liquidity**.<br>這個市場目前以持有高流動性資產為主流。 |

**lobby**
['lɑbɪ]
動
遊說

It's no big secret that the pharmaceutical industry is constantly **lobbying** governments around the world.
醫藥工業一直在遊說各國政府，這幾乎是公開的祕密。

**loom**
[lum]
動
逐漸發酵

In the distance, dark clouds **loomed** signaling that a storm was on the way.
烏雲在不遠處漸漸聚集，看來暴風雨快來了。

**loophole**
['lup,hol]
名
漏洞

Through a little-known legal **loophole**, the insurance company managed to avoid a payout.
靠著一些不為人知的法律漏洞，這間保險公司設法避免了一個理賠。

| | |
|---|---|
| **lull**<br>[lʌl]<br>名<br>停滯 | There's been a **lull** in activity on the stock market this week.<br>這個星期股票市場的交易呈現停滯的狀況。 |
| **majority**<br>[mə'dʒɔrətɪ]<br>名<br>大多數 | Lawmakers voted through the bill by a large **majority**.<br>立法委員在大多數同意的狀況下通過這個法案。 |
| **mentor**<br>[mɛntɚ]<br>名<br>良師益友 | Jack is more than just a good friend, he is also a **mentor** to me.<br>傑克對我而言不只是個益友，更是位良師。 |

| | |
|---|---|
| **militant**<br>['mɪlətənt]<br>形<br>好戰的；強勢的 | Rather than take a **militant** stance on political issues, Gertrude preferred to try to see things from all angles.<br>葛瑞琴並不願意在政治議題上採取強勢態度，她比較喜歡用各種不同角度看事情。 |
| **negligent**<br>['nɛglɪdʒənt]<br>形<br>疏忽的 | The parents were accused of being **negligent** after they left their kids alone for the entire day.<br>這對夫婦因為把孩子們單獨留在家中一整天，而被控告疏忽職責。 |
| **nonetheless**<br>[ˌnʌnðə'lɛs]<br>連<br>不過 | With all the things she has been through, this has been a difficult year for Natalie; **nonetheless**, she has remained upbeat.<br>娜塔麗經歷了這麼些事，今年對她而言真的很辛苦，但是，她仍然鼓起精神。 |

**offload**
['ɑflod]
動
卸貨

Don't try to **offload** those faulty computer games you bought on me. I'm not interested!
不用費心給我那些有瑕疵的電腦遊戲了。我沒有興趣。

**opponent**
[ə'ponənt]
名
對手

In days of old, kings would frequently get rid of any **opponents** to their rule.
在古時候，國王通常會除掉對他的統治有威脅的對手。

**outfit**
['aut͵fɪt]
名
衣服；裝備

Yolanda has had her eye on that **outfit** for some time, but I'm not sure whether she can afford it.
尤蘭達中意那件衣服好一陣子了，但我不知道她是否買得起。

**output**
['aut,put]
名
產量

The factory's **output** is lagging way behind demand meaning we can't meet our order promises.

這間工廠的產量目前遠低於需要量，也就是說我們無法達到我們的訂單承諾。

**outsource**
['aut,sors]
動
外包

By **outsourcing** customer services to developing countries like India, many corporations have drastically slashed overheads.

藉由把客服部門外包到發展中國家如印度，很多公司都大幅縮減了經常性的開銷。

**overflow**
[,ovə-'flo]
動
溢出

Following torrential rains, water **overflowed** from the banks of the river.

在幾場豪雨後，水衝破堤防滿出來了。

| | |
|---|---|
| **overhaul**<br>[ˌovɚˈhɔl]<br>形<br>大檢修 | We need to achieve a complete **overhaul** of our quality control procedures.<br>我們需要完成一次針對我們品質管制程序的大檢測。 |
| **overhead**<br>[ˌovɚˈhɛd]<br>副<br>在頭上 | Bats circled **overhead** giving the scene the atmosphere of a horror movie.<br>蝙蝠在頭上盤旋給了這個景象一種恐怖片的氣氛。 |
| **overshad-ow**<br>[ˌovɚˈʃædo]<br>動<br>籠罩陰影 | The festival should have been a joyful event, but it was **overshad-owed** by the deaths.<br>這個嘉年華會應該是個開心的活動，但是因為一些傷亡而覆蓋陰影。 |

| | |
|---|---|
| **plea**<br>[pli]<br>名<br>訴求 | Charities in East Africa have made a **plea** for help in tackling the famine that is ravaging the region.<br>東非的慈善機構呼籲援手，幫忙應付這個區域面臨的饑荒侵襲。 |
| **plead**<br>[plid]<br>動<br>請求 | Marlon **pleaded** with his mother to let him go to the party.<br>馬龍請求他的母親允許他去派對。 |
| **pledge**<br>[plɛdʒ]<br>動<br>質押，典當；付交 | It's really great that wealthy philanthropists like Bill Gates have **pledged** a portion of their fortune to charity.<br>像比爾蓋茲這類富有的慈善家將部分財產捐給慈善機構，是件很棒的事。 |

**plush**
[plʌʃ]
形
奢華的

Have you heard about Walter and Betty's **plush** new apartment in the Caribbean?
你有聽說瓦特和貝蒂在加樂比海的豪華公寓嗎？

**poise**
[pɔɪz]
名
姿勢

The ballet dancer combined elegance with almost perfect **poise**.
這位芭蕾舞者在他完美的舞姿中結合了優雅。

**posh**
[pɑʃ]
形
優雅漂亮的

That guy over there talks with a really **posh** accent.
那邊那位男士說話時有十分幽雅的口音。

| | |
|---|---|
| **pragmatic**<br>[præg'mætɪk]<br>形<br>務實的 | After a series of failed relationships, Julia decided she needed to take a more **pragmatic** approach to finding Mr. Right.<br>在幾段失敗的感情後，茱麗決定她要用更務實的方法來找尋白馬王子。 |
| **prescription**<br>[prɪ'skrɪpʃən]<br>名<br>處方 | Drugs that are available only by **prescription** in America can be bought over the counter in other countries.<br>有些在美國必須要醫生處方才買得到的藥，在其他國家可以在藥房櫃檯買到。 |
| **prior**<br>['praɪɚ]<br>形<br>之前的 | Without any **prior** experience in the field, Samantha knew she would be hard pushed to get the job.<br>因先前沒有任何相關的經驗，珊曼莎知道她必須更努力的得到這份工作。 |

| | |
|---|---|
| **proceeding**<br>[prə'sidɪŋ]<br>名<br>訴訟程式；進行 | All of the major newspapers in the city sent reporters to the court to cover the **proceedings** of the murder case.<br>城裡所有主流報紙都派了記者到法庭去掌握這個謀殺案的審判進行狀況。 |
| **pronouncement**<br>[prə'naunsmənt]<br>名<br>官方公告 | Otis is well-known for making ridiculous **pronouncements** on matters he knows nothing about.<br>歐提司在針對他完全不懂的事情上做荒謬的發言上是出了名的。 |
| **pundit**<br>['pʌndɪt]<br>名<br>權威 | Whatever the **pundits** say, I'm putting my money on the underdog to cause an upset in this match.<br>不管專家怎麼說，我都要把我的錢壓在這個居劣勢的人，來讓這場比賽多少令人沮喪。 |

| | |
|---|---|
| **radical**<br>['rædɪkl̩]<br>形<br>激進的 | Known for his **radical** opinions, the philosopher was considered an important thinker.<br>這位哲學家以想法激進聞名，被認為是一位十分重要的思想家。 |
| **rebate**<br>['ribet]<br>名<br>退款 | I was looking forward to a sizable tax **rebate** this year but ended up with nothing!<br>我一直期待會有大筆的退稅，但結果是一毛都沒有。 |
| **rebound**<br>['rɪbaund]<br>名<br>反彈 | I'm afraid to say, Amy is dating that guy purely because she is on the **rebound** from her last boyfriend.<br>我不得不說，愛咪之所以跟這個人約會只是一種對她前男友的反彈心理。 |

**rebound**
[rɪ'baund]
動
復甦

All the talk in the sports pages is about how the national team will **rebound** from this latest defeat.
這幾頁體育版的所有討論都是關於國家隊要如何從最近的挫敗中恢復士氣。

**rebuff**
[rɪ'bʌf]
動
斷然拒絕

Although I've offered my assistance several times, Fran keeps **rebuffing** me.
雖然我屢次表示可以協助，但法蘭還是斷然地拒絕我。

**redress**
[rɪ'drɛs]
動
補救

We're sorry for the problem with the service we provided and would like to do our best to **redress** the situation.
我們很遺憾我們提供的服務出問題，而且我們願意盡我們全力來補救這個狀況。

| | |
|---|---|
| **reduction**<br>[rɪ'dʌkʃən]<br>名<br>減少，降低 | Since my company has taken on more staff, I have experienced a welcome **reduction** in my workload.<br>自從公司引進較多員工後，我很開心我的工作負擔減少了。 |
| **reevaluate**<br>[ˌriɪ'væljuˌet]<br>動<br>重新評估 | After it was defeated in the election, the political party realized it would have to **reevaluate** its strategy.<br>這個政黨在選舉中失利後，他們瞭解必須重新評估策略。 |
| **reiterate**<br>[ri'ɪtəˌret]<br>動<br>重申 | Let me **reiterate** my position: I'm not going to put up with playing second fiddle in this partnership anymore.<br>請容我重申我的立場：我之後不會再在合夥權益上讓步了。 |

| | |
|---|---|
| **relevant**<br>['rɛləvənt]<br>形<br>有相關的 | Sorry, but I can't see how what you're saying is **relevant** to the topic in hand.<br>抱歉，但是我真的看不出來你所說的跟目前的主題有何相關連性。 |
| **resilient**<br>[rɪ'zɪlɪənt]<br>形<br>有活力的 | Children are often more **resilient** than one imagines.<br>孩子們總是超乎想像的有活力。 |
| **respective-ly**<br>[rɪ'spɛktɪvlɪ]<br>副<br>個別地 | In terms of languages spoken, the top two countries in the world are Papua New Guinea and Indonesia **respectively**.<br>以口語來說，全球前兩名的兩個國家分別是是巴布亞紐幾內亞和印尼。 |

**restore**
[rɪ'stor]
動
恢復

Once the riots spiraled out of control, there was talk of the army being called in to **restore** order.
一旦這個暴動擴散，據說會有武力進駐維持秩序。

**restraint**
[rɪ'strent]
名
克制

Even though Denise can be annoying, please show some **restraint** when you speak to her.
雖然迪尼絲真的讓人受不了，但是你跟她說話時還是克制一下吧！

**resurgence**
[rɪ'sɝdʒəns]
名
復甦

Certain trends die out only to see a **resurgence** in a later era.
某些趨勢消失但總是會在之後的某個時代復甦。

| | |
|---|---|
| **retain**<br>[rɪ'ten]<br>動<br>保留 | Authors submitting stories for use in this anthology will **retain** copyright over their work.<br>作者們把所寫的故事提供給這個選集使用後，他們仍然是故事的版權所有者。 |
| **reverberation**<br>[rɪ,vɝbə'reʃən]<br>名<br>回響、影響 | **Reverberations** from the rock concert could be heard throughout the area.<br>這場搖滾演場會的回音籠罩在這整個地區。 |
| **revive**<br>[rɪ'vaɪv]<br>動<br>重新流行 | Several pop groups have **revived** the trend for 50s rock and roll.<br>好幾個流行樂團重新翻唱了五零年代的搖滾樂。 |

**risk-free**
['rɪsk,fri]
形
零風險的

There's no such thing as a **risk-free** investment but I reckon this is a pretty safe bet.
世界上沒有任何零風險的投資，不過我知道這個投資是相對安全的。

**rural**
['rurəl]
形
郊區的

In most countries a move from **rural** to urban areas is a natural result of industrialization.
在大部分國家，從農村轉型到都市化是工業化的必然結果。

**salvage**
['sælvɪdʒ]
動
搶救

While we have lost a lot of business this year, with hard work, I am certain we can **salvage** something.
在我們今年流失很多生意之際，我仍堅信只要我們認真工作，一定可以亡羊補牢。

**scandal**
['skændl]
名
醜聞

There was no way back for the champion cyclist after the doping **scandal** tarnished his reputation beyond repair.
在毒品醜聞把這位單車賽車手冠軍的名譽詆毀後，要重返生涯是無望了。

**scope**
[skop]
名
槍的瞄準器；議程範圍

That's an interesting suggestion but it's not currently within the **scope** of this meeting.
那是個很有趣的建議，不過並不在這個會議的議程裡。

**scroll**
[skrol]
動
移動

**Scroll** down to the bottom of the screen and you'll see the news article I was talking about.
你往下看到螢幕的底部，就會看到我說的那個新聞報導。

**shield**
[ʃild]
名
板

Derek used his bag as a **shield** against the rain.
德瑞克用他的袋子當作遮雨的板子。

**skeptical**
['skɛptɪkl]
形
質疑的

To be honest, I'm **skeptical** about this contractor's ability to do a good job on this project.
老實說，我對於這個包商在執行這個工程上的能力存疑。

**slot**
[slɑt]
名
空缺

My university professor says he's all tied up this week but has a few **slots** available next Thursday.
我的大學教授說他這個星期都排滿了，不過下週四會有幾個時段有空。

| | |
|---|---|
| **sluggish**<br>['slʌgɪʃ]<br>形<br>遲緩的 | After a night on the town, James climbed out of bed around noon feeling rather **sluggish**.<br>出去玩一整晚後，詹姆士中午好不容易爬起床，但是還是感覺很懶散。 |
| **slump**<br>[slʌmp]<br>動<br>下降 | This third quarter has seen sales of the fashion brand's latest designs **slumping** by more than 20 percent.<br>第三季的銷售上已經看到這個時尚廠牌最新設計的銷售量下滑了百分之二十。 |
| **stagnation**<br>[stæg'neʃən]<br>名<br>不景氣 | Although the economy has suffered a sustained spell of **stagnation**, there is reason to be optimistic about a change for the better.<br>儘管經濟狀況目前面臨不景氣，還是有足夠理由讓我們對改善抱持樂觀的態度。 |

| | |
|---|---|
| **standoff**<br>['stænd,ɔf]<br>名<br>對峙 | The **standoff** between the hostage taker and the police continued for 30 hours.<br>控制人質的罪犯和警察的對峙持續了三十分鐘。 |
| **stockpile**<br>['stɑk,paɪl]<br>動<br>囤積 | North Korea has frequently been accused of **stockpiling** weapons by the West.<br>北韓一直被西方國家指控囤積武器。 |
| **strap**<br>[stræp]<br>名<br>帶子 | Little more than a week after I bought this bag, the **strap** on it broke.<br>我買了這個袋子之後一個多星期，它的背帶就斷了。 |

| | |
|---|---|
| **strategy**<br>['strætədʒɪ]<br>名<br>策略 | Forced to confront the truth that his **strategy** had failed, the manager resigned from his position.<br>被迫面對了他的策略失敗這個事實，這位經理辭掉了他的職位。 |
| **streamline**<br>['strim,laɪn]<br>動<br>提高效率 | Employees filed for unfair dismissal with the labor affairs bureau after the **streamlining** measures at the company left them redundant.<br>由於公司執行了提高效率的政策讓員工被解聘，所以員工群起向勞工局抗議所受的不平待遇。 |
| **struggling**<br>['strʌgl̩ɪŋ]<br>形<br>並不走紅的 | Many **struggling** small businesses go under within a year of being established.<br>很多經營不善的小生意在剛開始的一年內就面臨破產。 |

| | |
|---|---|
| **susceptibility**<br>[sə,sɛptə'bɪlətɪ]<br>形<br>易患的；敏感的 | Sharp changes of temperature can increase one's **susceptibility** to colds and the flu.<br>氣溫的極端變化很容易引起著涼或是感冒。 |
| **suspenseful**<br>[sə'spɛnsfəl]<br>形<br>緊張刺激的 | At the end of the Western movie, there was a **suspenseful** showdown between the hero and the bad guy.<br>在這部西部片的最後，是一場緊張刺激的英雄與壞人大對決橋段。 |
| **sustainable**<br>[sə'stenəbl]<br>形<br>有支撐力的 | Economists are unsure if the country's growth is **sustainable** in the long term.<br>經濟學家不確定這個國家的成長在長期而言是否穩健。 |

| | |
|---|---|
| **swamp**<br>[swamp]<br>動<br>窮於應付 | Jeanette claimed she couldn't help me proofread the report as she was **swamped** with her own projects.<br>珍娜說她沒辦法幫我校對報告，因為她自己手邊的案子都忙不完了。 |
| **tension**<br>['tɛnʃən]<br>名<br>緊張的氣氛 | The **tension** was so thick during the chess match that you could cut it with a knife.<br>在這場棋奕比賽中緊張的氣氛非常濃厚，好像可以用刀切開一樣。 |
| **tenure**<br>['tɛnjur]<br>名<br>任期 | Most of us were sad to hear the professor's **tenure** as head of the philosophy department was drawing to a close.<br>我們大部分人對於教授在哲學系系主任的任期即將屆滿都感到遺憾。 |

| | |
|---|---|
| **tough**<br>[tʌf]<br>形<br>較困難的 | Growing up on the wrong side of the tracks, Delbert had had a **tough** life.<br>在錯誤的成長過程中，達爾伯特的一生很辛苦。 |
| **tribute**<br>['trɪbjut]<br>名<br>貢獻，進貢 | There's a concert in the park this weekend to pay **tribute** to the famous rights activist.<br>這個週末在公園裡有個演唱會，是對有名的人權鬥士的致敬。 |
| **tribunal**<br>[traɪ'bjunl̩]<br>名<br>法庭 | A **tribunal** is to be set up to investigate the accusations of malpractice by the media outlet.<br>一個法庭最近被成立來調查這個針對媒體報導的一個醫生誤診的指控。 |

| | |
|---|---|
| **tricky**<br>['trɪkɪ]<br>形<br>微妙的；有陷阱的 | Did you manage to solve those **tricky** math problems the teacher assigned us for homework?<br>你解出老師出給我們寫的那些難解的數學作業嗎？ |
| **tweak**<br>[twik]<br>動<br>強化 | The inventor was on the verge of completing his new innovation but just needed to **tweak** the design here and there.<br>這位發明家的發明已經接近完成，現在只需要在設計上做些加強。 |
| **underesti-mate**<br>['ʌndɚ'ɛstəmet]<br>動<br>低估 | One should never **underestimate** the influence a person's upbringing has on their personality.<br>一個人的成長過程對個性的影響是不該被低估的。 |

| | |
|---|---|
| **union**<br>['junjən]<br>名<br>公會 | Civil servants in many countries are prevented from forming **unions** to safeguard their work rights.<br>公務員在很多國家是不可以組成工會來保護他們的工作權的。 |
| **unleash**<br>[ʌn'liʃ]<br>動<br>解開鏈子；釋放 | The boxer **unleashed** a barrage of ferocious blows to knock out his opponent.<br>這位拳擊手展開了一連串猛烈的攻擊來把他的對手打倒。 |
| **upgrade**<br>['ʌp'gred]<br>名<br>升級 | I still have gotten around to installing that software **upgrade** for my media player.<br>我還沒有時間可以把我的媒體播放器裡的軟體升級。 |

| | |
|---|---|
| **upturn**<br>[ʌp'tɝn]<br>名<br>反轉 | An **upturn** in social order was a natural result of the collapse of the government.<br>社會秩序的反轉是政府崩潰後的必然結果。 |
| **validate**<br>['vælə͵det]<br>名<br>生效 | To **validate** this visa, you need to have it stamped at the immigration counter down the hall.<br>要讓簽證生效，你必須到大廳那個移民櫃檯蓋章。 |
| **veteran**<br>[vɛtərən]<br>名<br>退伍軍人 | Many war **veterans** return home with deep psychological scars as a result of their experiences.<br>很多退伍軍人在回鄉後都有很多源自戰時經驗導致的精神創傷。 |

| | |
|---|---|
| **vigilant**<br>['vɪdʒələnt]<br>形<br>警覺性的 | You'd better be **vigilant** with your possessions around here at night as there are some shady characters walking the streets.<br>你晚上在這區走路要小心你的隨身物品，因為有些宵小在附近街上遊蕩。 |
| **vital**<br>['vaɪtḷ]<br>形<br>重要的 | A comfortable work environment and good posture are **vital** to avoid back problems.<br>一個舒適的工作環境以及正面的態度，對避免日後的問題是非常重要的。 |
| **volunteer**<br>[͵vɑlən'tɪr]<br>名<br>志願者，義工 | Without **volunteers**, the charity would have difficulty continuing to function.<br>在沒有義工的狀況下，慈善團體會面臨繼續營運的困境。 |

| | |
|---|---|
| **yield**<br>[jild]<br>動<br>獲利 | Check out this article that I'm reading concerning high **yield** stocks that continue to reap dividends year after year.<br>你看看我現在在念的這篇有關高獲利股票的文章，它們每年都有持續獲利。 |
| **yield**<br>[jild]<br>動<br>讓路 | Nothing bugs me more than drivers who refuse to **yield** to pedestrians.<br>最讓我無法忍受的事是司機拒絕讓路給行人。 |

# 02/ 新多益必考片語列表

Note

| | |
|---|---|
| **(a bunch of) hot air**<br>大話，空話 | Our boss lectured us for nearly an hour about changes to company policy, but most of us felt it was just **a bunch of hot air**.<br>我們老闆念了我們將近一個小時關於公司政策的改變，可是我們大部分人都覺得是在說大話。 |
| **a clean slate**<br>重新開始 | Now that I'm in charge of operations here, I'm prepared to forget what may have happened in the past and give everyone **a clean slate**.<br>現在這裡由我來執掌營運，我有心理準備要忘記以前的一切讓大家都重新開始。 |
| **a lot riding on (something)**<br>很倚重某件事 | We have **a lot riding on** this account, so let's make sure we do our best.<br>我們非常需要這個客戶，所以讓我們確認有盡全力吧。 |

| | |
|---|---|
| **a mountain of (something)**<br>很多的 | Sorry, but I won't be able to make it to the party on Friday as I have **a mountain of** work that needs finishing.<br>抱歉，我無法參加這週五的聚會，因為我有好多工作待完成。 |
| **a windfall in**<br>意外之財 | Alistair was convinced his investments would reap **a windfall in** profits over the next few years.<br>阿利思達確信他的投資在接下來的幾年會帶給他很好的獲利。 |
| **all out**<br>全部的 | We need to go **all out** if we are to have any hope of securing the contract with this client.<br>如果我們想確保和這個客戶的合約，我們必須得竭盡全力才行。 |

| | |
|---|---|
| **along the same lines**<br>同樣的方向 | My friend really liked the Website you built me and was wondering if you do something **along the same lines** for him.<br>我的朋友真的很喜歡你幫我做的這個網站，他想知道你可不可以也幫他做一個一樣的。 |
| **as of late**<br>最近，目前 | I've noticed you don't have much time on your hands **as of late**.<br>我注意到你最近很忙，都沒有自己的時間。 |
| **as pleased as punch**<br>非常開心 | I'm **as pleased as punch** that you made it to my speech.<br>你能夠來我的演講，我真的非常開心。 |

| | |
|---|---|
| **at the risk of**<br>冒…危險 | **At the risk of** sounding rude, I'd appreciate it if you could keep your opinions to yourself in the future.<br>我冒著出言不遜的危險跟你說，如果你以後可以不要跟我分享你的意見，我會很感激。 |
| **bail out**<br>緊急援助 | While I had to work my way through college, my housemates had the luxury of knowing their parents would **bail** them **out** if they were short of cash.<br>當我想盡辦法念完大學之際，我的樓友則揮霍無度，因為他知道如果沒錢了，他的父母會資助他。 |
| **ballpark figure**<br>大約的數字 | Give me a **ballpark figure** before we proceed with negotiations.<br>我們進行協商前，請給我一個大約的數字。 |

| | |
|---|---|
| **bang for the buck**<br>值回票價，划算；滿意 | These sneakers I picked up from the outlet store last week are really **bang for the buck** compared to the last pair I bought.<br>跟我上次買的那一雙球鞋比起來，我上星期在賣場買的真的是太划算了。 |
| **bank on**<br>依賴，信賴 | I wouldn't **bank on** her changing her mind about helping you after the way you spoke to her last time.<br>在你上次跟她說那樣的話之後。我不敢指望她還會改變主意幫助你。 |
| **beat (someone) at (some-body's) own game**<br>以其人之道還治其人之身 | Having been taken advantage of by the major corporations for years, the OEM decided to take them on and **beat** them **at** their **own game**.<br>在被大集團佔便宜數年後，這間代工的公司決定要以其人之道還治其身。 |

| | |
|---|---|
| **before (time) is out**<br>在…結束前 | Please complete that report and have it on my desk **before** the week **is out**.<br>請在週末前把報告完成，並且放在我的桌上。 |
| **bend to the will**<br>態度向…傾斜 | I'm sick of having to **bend to the will** of my manager on every issue, especially when she is clearly wrong.<br>我受夠了總是要在每件議題上都要聽我的經理的，尤其當她很明顯是錯誤的時候。 |
| **big time**<br>大勝；顛峰 | Before he hit the **big time**, the actor had struggled for recognition for many years.<br>在這位演員達到顛峰前，他有好幾年時間都在辛苦地尋求認同。 |

| | |
|---|---|
| **black and white**<br>明確的定律 | The issue is by no means **black and white** but actually a great deal more complicated than you might imagine.<br>這個議題看來十分明確簡單，但事實上它的複雜是你無法想像的。 |
| **blame (some-body)**<br>埋怨 | I tried to wake you up, so don't **blame** me if you're late for work.<br>我有試著叫你起床，如果你上班遲到不要怪我哦！ |
| **bottom line**<br>底限 | We won't agree to anything less than a 40 percent share in the profits of this venture, and that is the **bottom line**.<br>我們不會同意任何在這個合作案中低於百分之四十的獲利分攤，這是底限。 |

| | |
|---|---|
| **brace for**<br>防備 | In light of the recent weather reports, we're all **bracing** ourselves **for** a cold winter this year.<br>根據最近的天氣報導，我們都在防備迎接今年寒冷的冬天。 |
| **break the back of**<br>筋疲力盡（工作過度） | In the 1980s, the British Prime Minister Margaret Thatcher **broke the back of** the mining unions.<br>在1980年代，英國首相柴契爾夫人讓礦工聯盟辛苦工作。 |
| **bring forth**<br>帶出；引起；提及 | The argument between the sisters **brought forth** many long-standing issues that had never been resolved.<br>這幾位姊妹間的爭吵，也帶出了長期沒有解決的問題。 |

| | |
|---|---|
| **bring (someone) on board**<br>引薦某人進入公司 | An independent legal adviser has been **brought on board** to ensure that we are doing everything by the book.<br>一位獨立的法律顧問進駐公司，來確保我們有照章行事。 |
| **bring up the rear**<br>殿後；業績落後 | Look down there and you can see them coming up the mountain with Sally in front, then Jeremy, Scott and, finally, Yasmine **bringing up the rear**.<br>你往下看，可以看到他們從山下上來，莎莉走第一，之後是傑若米、史考特，而雅斯敏殿後。 |
| **building block**<br>磚塊；基石 | By fostering industrialization in developing countries, the agency said it was providing the **building blocks** of a better future.<br>這間公司說藉由在發展中國家促進工業發展，他們同時也為了未來奠定基礎。 |

| | |
|---|---|
| **bum out**<br>洩氣 | What's wrong with Fred these days? He always looks tired and **bummed out.**<br>佛萊德最近怎麼了？他總是看起來很累而且很洩氣的樣子。 |
| **carbon footprint**<br>碳足跡 | Pacific island nations are among the lowest polluters in the world and, as a result, leave a very faint **carbon footprint.**<br>太平洋島國是世界上汙染源最少的國家，所以他們也造成極輕微的碳足跡。 |
| **catch (someone's) breath**<br>喘口氣 | Marty is not in good shape like his tennis partner and often has to **catch** his **breath** in between points when they play.<br>馬帝體力不如他的網球球伴好，他們打球時，他經常必須要在分數間休息一下，喘口氣。 |

| | |
|---|---|
| **catch up on**<br>趕上 | I can't wait to meet up this weekend and **catch up on** all the latest gossip.<br>我好期待這個週末的聚會，可以好好敘敘舊聊八卦。 |
| **check out**<br>視察；了解 | Let's go to the art gallery tomorrow to **check out** that new exhibition.<br>我們明天去藝廊看看新的展覽吧！ |
| **chip in**<br>分擔金錢〔工作〕 | The restaurant is short staffed today, so even the manager is **chipping in** to share the workload.<br>餐廳今天人手不足，連經理都幫忙分擔工作。 |

| | |
|---|---|
| **civil suit**<br>民事訴訟 | After the criminal case against the suspect collapsed, the prosecution filed a **civil suit**.<br>在對嫌犯的刑事訴訟敗訴後，檢方決定以民事上訴。 |
| **clean out of**<br>用完了 | As the local store is **clean out of** margarine, we'll have to go to the supermarket for it.<br>當小店的人造奶油賣完了，我們就必須去超市買了。 |
| **clear sailing (ahead)**<br>前途無礙 | The first part of this hike is pretty challenging, but after that it's **clear sailing** for the rest of the way.<br>這次爬山一開始還蠻辛苦的〔具挑戰性〕，不過後來就輕鬆了。 |

| | |
|---|---|
| **cluster graph**<br>群集圖 | The physicist represented her findings using a **cluster graph**.<br>這位物理學家利用一個群集圖來呈現她的發現。 |
| **contend with**<br>滿足；應付 | Teachers have enough to **contend with** without having to be social workers for children as well.<br>老師們應該滿足於他們的工作中，不需要還充當社工照顧孩子。 |
| **contingent on**<br>視…狀況而定 | Whether or not Josie passes the exam is **contingent on** how much effort he decides to put in.<br>荷西是否可以通過考試，端賴於他要多努力。 |

| | |
|---|---|
| **cool head**<br>冷靜 | Regardless of the amount of pressure that was heaped on his shoulders, Javier always managed to keep a **cool head**.<br>儘管哈維爾有很多的壓力，他總是還是設法保持冷靜。 |
| **cost-cutting measures**<br>降低成本的方法 | To have any chance of maintaining profitability, we're going to have to implement some stringent **cost-cutting measures** from now on.<br>除了要掌握任何可以維持利潤的方法之外，我們現在開始也要嚴格執行一些降低成本的方案。 |
| **debit card**<br>銀行卡 | **Debit cards** are handy, but they can't be used for all online purchases.<br>銀行卡是蠻好用的，但是不適用於所有的線上購物。 |

| | |
|---|---|
| **down-and-out**<br>窮困潦倒的 | Until you've been **down-and-out** you'll never really understand what poverty is like.<br>除非你真的窮困潦倒過，不然你是無法真正體會窮困是什麼。 |
| **doze off**<br>打瞌睡 | The teacher gave Ralph an earful after he noticed him **dozing off** at the back of the classroom.<br>老師發現羅夫坐在教室後面打瞌睡，就好好地訓了他一頓。 |
| **dress code**<br>服裝規定 | I'll have to buy a suit for the function as the **dress code** on the invitation says smart.<br>因為邀請函上的規定，我必須要買一套西裝以出席宴會。 |

| | |
|---|---|
| **dumping ground**<br>垃圾場 | Stray dogs scavenged through the garbage in the **dumping ground** on the edge of the city.<br>流浪狗在在市區旁的垃圾堆裡翻找食物。 |
| **easy come, easy go**<br>來得快，去得快 | Patrick gave me that camera, so I felt it was a case of **easy come, easy go** when I lost it.<br>派崔克給我那臺相機，所以當我弄丟它時，我只感覺到這就是來得容易，去得也快的最佳寫照。 |
| **economic climate**<br>經濟景氣狀況 | In the present **economic climate**, expansion into foreign markets is not advised.<br>在目前的經濟景氣狀況下，不建議拓展到海外市場。 |

| | |
|---|---|
| **emerging markets**<br>新興市場 | Rather than export to established Western economies, the textile firm focused on tapping into **emerging markets**.<br>這間紡織公司不想出口到成熟的西方經濟體，而將焦點放在新興市場。 |
| **experience under (somebody's) belt**<br>很多經驗 | With so many years of **experience under** my **belt**, I think I have a good chance of getting this position.<br>有著這麼多年的經驗，我覺得我蠻有勝算可以得到這個職位。 |
| **facial gesture**<br>臉部表情 | It's often hard to gauge the meaning of **facial gestures** from people in cultures that are very different from your own.<br>要瞭解與自己不同文化的人的臉部表情的意義通常是不容易的。 |

| | |
|---|---|
| **fall flat**<br>未達預期效果 | My colleague is full of suggestions at our weekly meetings, but they invariably **fall flat**.<br>我的同事在週會議上提出很多建議，可是它們都沒有達到效果。 |

| | |
|---|---|
| **figure in the equation**<br>考慮的因素 | Some of these service providers shouldn't even **figure in the equation** when we discuss who to outsource the project to.<br>我們在討論要把案子外包給哪一家時，有一些競標廠商條件太差，甚至不該被列入考慮。 |

| | |
|---|---|
| **financial arm**<br>財務部門 | The **financial arm** of our firm is located in a different part of town.<br>我們公司的財務部門在城裡另一個地方。 |

| | |
|---|---|
| **first thing**<br>第一件做的事 | Once I receive details of the time and location of the conference, I'll call you **first thing**.<br>我一旦收到關於會議的時間和地點的細節時，我馬上就打電話給你。 |
| **fly off the shelves**<br>創造銷售佳績 | Every time a new game in that series is released, it simply **flies off the shelves**.<br>每一次這個系列的新遊戲上市，就馬上創造銷售佳績。 |
| **for starters**<br>首先 | If we are going to clear out some of the clutter in this house, I think we should get rid of that old bookcase **for starters**.<br>如果我們要把家裡整頓一下，那我想我們首先應該先把那個舊書架給丟了。 |

| | |
|---|---|
| **for the time being**<br>目前 | Can we put that issue aside **for the time being** and move to the next item on the agenda?<br>我們可以把那一項議題先擱一旁，先進行議程裡的下一項嗎？ |
| **gear to**<br>投注於 | Our latest line of sportswear is **geared to** a more mature market.<br>我們最新的運動服的產品線主要客群投注在較成熟的族群。 |
| **get down to brass tacks**<br>事實真相 | Now that we've agreed on the basics, let's **get down to brass tacks** and discuss what kind of price we're talking about for this project.<br>現在我們針對基本條件達成協議了，我們應該回歸事件本身，來討論這個案子的價錢了。 |

| | |
|---|---|
| **get off the ground**<br>營運起飛 | Before we think about our long term targets, we need to **get** this project **off the ground** first.<br>在我們思考我們長期的目標前，我們應該要先讓這個案子開始起跑。 |
| **get one's ducks in a row**<br>條理分明 | Now that you're no longer a child, it's time you stopped acting irresponsibly and **got** your **ducks in a row**.<br>你現在不是小孩子了，你應該不要再不負責任，而要凡事條理分明了。 |
| **get (someone) up to speed**<br>讓（某人）瞭解 | Our new colleague is a little overwhelmed with having to learn so many things in such a short space of time, but we'll soon **get** her **up to speed**.<br>我們的新同事對於一下子要學這麼多東西有點無法招架，不過我們很快會幫助她上軌道的。 |

| | |
|---|---|
| **get (something) ironed out**<br>處理好 | We need to **get** the remaining issues over production **ironed out** by the end of this week.<br>在這個週末前，我們必須把生產方面剩下的問題都解決。 |
| **get (something) sorted out**<br>弄清楚 | Please **get** this **sorted out** before it becomes problematic.<br>在這件事成為問題前，請先把它搞清楚。 |
| **get to the bottom of (something)**<br>追根究底 | Investigators have no leads yet but have vowed to **get to the bottom of** the bank robbery.<br>調查員目前還沒有任何的線索，可是他們誓言要對這個銀行搶案追根究底。 |

| | |
|---|---|
| **go the extra mile**<br>多盡一些力 | Unlike other luxury hotels in the region, we **go the extra mile** to ensure customer satisfaction.<br>比起這一區其他豪華的飯店，我們在確保顧客滿意上更盡心盡力。 |
| **go with**<br>決定要買〔取得〕 | Of all the logo designs we've considered, this is obviously the most popular, so we'll just **go with** that.<br>在眾多我們考慮過的商標中，這個顯然是最受歡迎的，所以我們要使用這個。 |
| **goof off**<br>打混 | Nick is always **goofing off** at work, but somehow he seems to get away with it.<br>尼克總是在上班時打混，可是不知怎地他總能全身而退。 |

| | |
|---|---|
| **hands-on**<br>親手的，親自的 | Rather than delegate all the work to his employees, Jason always assumed a **hands-on** role as a manager.<br>雖身為經理，但傑森總是喜歡事必躬親，不會把所有的工作都指派給他的員工。 |
| **hang (someone) out to dry**<br>讓…身陷危險〔麻煩〕 | You really **hung** me **out to dry** by refusing to cover for me when the manager asked where I was earlier on.<br>經理剛剛問我在哪裡時你拒絕掩護我，真是存心讓我有麻煩。 |
| **hard cash**<br>現金 | The car dealer agreed to cut me a deal if I paid in **hard cash**.<br>車商答應如果我用現金交易就給我折扣。 |

| | |
|---|---|
| **have it your way**<br>照自己意思做 | I was only trying to help but it's fine if you don't want to follow my advice. **Have it your way**!<br>我只是試著幫忙，不過如果你不想接受我的建議也沒關係。你就照你自己的意思吧！ |
| **hire out**<br>出租 | So many landlords are **hiring out** office space these days that we should be able to find a good location downtown.<br>很多屋主都在出租辦公室，我們應該可以在市區找到一個好地方。 |
| **hold a grudge**<br>懷恨在心；心存芥蒂 | I can't believe Sheila still **holds a grudge** over the argument we had months ago.<br>我無法相信席拉到現在還針對我們幾個月前的爭執心存芥蒂。 |

| | |
|---|---|
| **hold in high esteem**<br>備受尊崇 | Nelson Mandela is **held in high esteem** by people around the world for his statesmanship and battle against injustice.<br>曼德拉是受全世界尊崇的人，因為他的政治風範和勇於抗爭不公。 |
| **hold your horses**<br>慢點 | We haven't even finished discussing the first stage of the project yet, so please **hold your horses**!<br>我們連這個案子的第一個階段都還沒討論，所以請你慢一點。 |
| **hostile takeover**<br>惡意接收企業 | Several high-profile redundancies followed the **hostile takeover** of the firm.<br>繼公司被惡意接收後，隨之而來的是幾次的大幅裁員。 |

| | |
|---|---|
| **hover around**<br>走來走去，盤旋 | The editor-in-chief is always **hovering around** in the background when it gets close to deadline time.<br>每當截稿日要到了，總編就會在背後走來走去。 |
| **if (somebody) so desires**<br>喜歡 | We can alter the font and background colors on the layout for this page, **if** you **so desire**.<br>如果你想要的話，我們在這一頁的設計上可以改變字體和背景顏色。 |
| **in a [the] (adj.) capacity**<br>地位；職位 | The vice-president made it clear that he was taking on the role of CEO **in a** temporary **capacity** only.<br>副總明確的表示他只是暫代公司裡執行長的職務。 |

| | |
|---|---|
| **in conjunction with**<br>合作；結合 | This presentation is brought to you **in conjunction with** our sponsors.<br>這個提案是結合了我們的贊助廠商一起提供給您的。 |
| **in droves**<br>成群結隊 | That new nightclub downtown is so popular that they are turning people away **in droves** most Saturdays.<br>市區裡那間夜總會好受歡迎，每到週六人們就會集結在那裡。 |
| **in full swing**<br>熱烈進行；激戰 | A movement to recognize the scientist's historical importance is now **in full swing**.<br>針對這位科學家的歷史重要性的認可的運動正在熱烈展開。 |

| | |
|---|---|
| **in jeopardy**<br>有危機 | Tom's weak performance at the interview has put his chances of landing the job **in jeopardy**.<br>湯姆在面試時差強人意的表現，讓他在得到這份工作上有危機。 |
| **in light of**<br>按照，根據，由於 | **In light of** the recent disaster, the airline vowed to undertake a comprehensive inquiry into what went wrong.<br>由於近期的災難，這家航空公司誓言要展開一個調查，瞭解問題所在。 |
| **in the balance**<br>平衡的 | The merger deal between the two firms remains **in the balance** until it receives approval by the board of directors.<br>這兩間公司的合併案目前不確定，等待董事會的同意。 |

| | |
|---|---|
| **in the wings**<br>在會議室旁的等候室；廂房；虎視眈眈地 | Tom was under serious pressure at work as he knew that, if he didn't perform, there were other people waiting **in the wings** to take over.<br>湯姆在工作上總是感到極度的壓力，而且他知道，如果他表現不好，旁邊有人等著要他的位子。 |
| **is (someone's) forte**<br>專長〔領域〕 | John likes to speak his mind and it's obvious that diplomacy **is**n't his **forte**.<br>約翰喜歡發表意見，不過他還真不太擅長辭令。 |
| **jump start**<br>快速展開 | The advertising firm **jump started** its campaign for the new line of children's clothing with a particularly memorable commercial.<br>這間廣告公司用了一個讓人印象深刻的廣告來配合這個新的童裝系列的上市。 |

| | |
|---|---|
| **keep (someone) abreast of**<br>讓（某人）知悉 | It's important to **keep abreast of** the latest developments in the industry.<br>熟知產業裡的最新發展是非常重要的。 |
| **keep (someone) posted**<br>讓人知道進度 | I'll miss Susan while she's away traveling, but she has promised to **keep** us **posted** about all her adventures.<br>當蘇珊去旅遊時我會想她的，不過她有承諾會隨時讓我們知道她的冒險。 |
| **kick off**<br>展開 | What time does the meeting **kick off** this afternoon? I need to know if I can make it back on time.<br>會議今天下午幾點開始？ 我要知道我趕不趕得回來。 |

| | |
|---|---|
| **kick the bucket**<br>過世 | There are so many things I want to have achieved before I **kick the bucket**!<br>在我一生結束前，我還有好多事想要達成呢！ |
| **knock off**<br>收工，下班 | We usually **knock off** for lunch at around 12:30 and the next hour is the only break we get at work.<br>我們通常是在12點半午餐休息，接下來的一個小時是我們忙碌工作中唯一可以休息的時間。 |
| **last-minute**<br>緊急的 | Please, let's not have any **last-minute** changes to the plans, OK?<br>拜託，我們不要有任何最後一分鐘的〔緊急的〕計畫改變好嗎？ |

| | |
|---|---|
| **lay the foundation**<br>建立基礎 | The efforts of the activists **laid the foundation** for democracy in the country.<br>在民運人士的努力下，奠定了這個國家的民主基礎。 |
| **let (someone) go**<br>讓某人離開 | Cutbacks at the factory were unavoidable and a decision was taken to **let** hundreds of staff **go**.<br>工廠的縮編是無可避免的，同時也必須決定遣散數百位職員。 |
| **live high on [off] the hog**<br>浮奢的 | While Bridgette was struggling to make ends meet, her elder sister had been **living high off the hog** for years.<br>當布莉姬辛苦地過日子時，她的姊姊卻奢華度日了好幾年。 |

| | |
|---|---|
| **lock up for**<br>囚禁 | The guilty verdict has been delivered by the jury, and the man is certain to be **locked up for** at least 20 years.<br>陪審團傳達了有罪的判決，這個人確定要被關上最少20年。 |
| **look at (someone) funny**<br>不解的 | Why is that fellow in the corner of the bar **looking** at me **funny**?<br>坐在酒吧角落那個傢伙為什麼用著不解的眼光看我？ |
| **lose sight of**<br>忽略 | We can't afford to **lose sight of** our targets if we are to increase profits this year.<br>如果我們今年要增加營收，我們就不能忽略我們的目標。 |

| | |
|---|---|
| **lowest [highest] rungs of**<br>最低階〔最高階〕 | I started out on the **lowest rungs of** the corporation but quickly made strides.<br>我從公司的最底層做起，但是很快地就升職。 |
| **make hay while the sun shines**<br>打鐵趁熱〔把握時機〕 | The older you get, the more difficult it is to learn a language, so **make hay while the sun shines.**<br>隨著年紀日長，學習語言會越難。所以要打鐵趁熱，把握學習的最佳時機。 |
| **make sense**<br>合理 | I can barely **make sense** of what Wanda says half the time.<br>幾乎一半的時間理我都不懂汪達要表達什麼。 |

| | |
|---|---|
| **market is saturated**<br>市場飽和 | I don't think opening a cram school in Taiwan is a great idea at the moment as the **market is saturated**.<br>我不覺得目前在臺灣開補習班是個好主意，因為市場已經飽和了。 |
| **mess up**<br>搞砸 | Having been given a second chance, Teddy promised not to **mess up** again.<br>被賦予第二次的機會，泰迪保證不會再搞砸了。 |
| **mind your P's and Q's**<br>做好本分 | Roland's mother is very prim and proper, so you had better **mind your P's and Q's** around her.<br>羅蘭的母親很一板一眼、沒有彈性，所以我勸你在她面前要本分一點。 |

| | |
|---|---|
| **more than welcome**<br>敬請；非常歡迎 | You're **more than welcome** to join us on the fishing trip if you're at a loose end.<br>如果你有空，我們非常歡迎你加入我們的釣魚之旅。 |
| **move up the corporate ladder**<br>升職 | The entrepreneur's autobiography explained how he **moved up the corporate ladder** to become one of the most powerful men in the industry.<br>這位企業創辦人的自傳裡寫到了他如何在公司的職位竄升到成為這個行業裡舉足輕重的人物。 |
| **mull over**<br>仔細評量 | Before we can come to an agreement we'll have to **mull over** some of the details in your offer.<br>在我們達成協議前，我們必須要針對你的提議仔細考慮一下。 |

| | |
|---|---|
| **null and void** 無效的 | Any breach of the contract will render it **null and void**. 任何違反合約的事情都會讓它無效。 |
| **off-putting** 令人卻步 | Sid loved the look of the motorbike but found the price **off-putting**. 席德喜歡這部摩托車的外型，可是他發現價格令人卻步。 |
| **off the charts** 超過；破表 | That guy seems so smart that his IQ must be **off the charts**. 這個人好像很厲害哦，他的智商一定破表。 |

**off the ground**
開始進行

Construction on the new subway line was delayed several times before finally getting **off the ground**.
這條新路線的地鐵工程在數度延期後才真正地開始建造。

**on an even keel**
穩定

My life had been nothing but late nights and parties for years, but since I got married, things have been **on an even keel**.
我的生活之前只有夜生活和派對，但自從我結婚後，一切都穩定了。

**on the eve of**
在⋯的前夕

**On the eve of** his wedding, Mike was taken out partying by his friends.
在麥克的婚禮前夕，他被朋友帶出去狂歡了。

**on the fritz [blink]**
壞掉了

For the third time this week the office photocopier is **on the fritz** again.

這是辦公室裡的影印機這個星期第三次壞掉了。

**on the whole**
整體而言

Education in the country was of a decent standard **on the whole**.

整體而言，這個國家的教育處於一個很好的狀況。

**once and for all**
一次解決

When the pop star won his legal case against the newspaper, it put paid to the rumors about his life (for) **once and for all**.

當這個流行巨星在這個法律案子上告贏了報社，他一次解決了謠言對他生活的影響。

| | |
|---|---|
| **open the floor up to**<br>開放接受意見表達 | I would now like to **open the floor up to** questions from our audience.<br>我現在想要開放，接受所有觀眾的提問。 |
| **pare down**<br>減少 | Moving into a much smaller apartment across town meant Christophe had to **pare down** his possessions.<br>搬到市區另一頭一間比較小的公寓意味著克里司多夫必須要減少他的東西。 |
| **pay lip service to**<br>光說不練 | Don only **pays lip service to** wanting to help out, whereas Eleanor really follows through on her promises.<br>唐總是只嘴上說說要幫忙，不過愛琳諾倒是真的坐到承諾幫忙。 |

| | |
|---|---|
| **pay off**<br>值得〔值回〕票價 | Herbie's weeks of training **paid off** when he came in first in the school swimming race.<br>當荷比在學校的游泳比賽得第一名時，他覺得數週的訓練值回票價了。 |
| **people in high places**<br>上流階層 | Without knowing some **people in high places**, I wouldn't have secured funding for my business.<br>我無法找到資金挹注我的公司，因為我沒有認識上流階層有錢的人士。 |
| **(person) of means**<br>有手段的 | He was born into a wealthy family and has always been a **person of means.**<br>他出生於富裕的家庭，而且他一直是個有手腕的人。 |

| | |
|---|---|
| **plunge into**<br>陷入 | Tough times and a series of bad moves by the owners **plunged** the restaurant chain **into** financial dire straits.<br>由於時機不好和老闆一連串的錯誤的行事，讓這連鎖餐廳陷入了財務上可怕的困境。 |
| **pour money into**<br>投資錢在… | The directors of the soccer team have **poured money into** the club without seeing any return for many years now.<br>已經好多年了，這支足球隊的經理一直把錢投資在這個俱樂部裡，但沒有回收。 |
| **precious little**<br>很珍貴的；很少 | You've got **precious little** right to speak to me like that.<br>你沒什麼資格可以這樣跟我說話。 |

| | |
|---|---|
| **prepared statement** 準備好的聲明 | The defendant in the court case issued a **prepared statement** to the media, which was read out by his lawyer.<br>法庭上的被告準備了一篇聲明稿給媒體，由他的律師念出來。 |
| **profits be squeezed** 獲益緊縮 | **Profits** from the recent sale of the subsidiary have **been squeezed** to the point where there is nothing left for reinvestment.<br>從子公司所來的獲益緊縮到沒有剩餘資金可以重新投資了。 |
| **profligate use of energy** 浪費資源 | Western powers have long been associated with **profligate use of energy**.<br>西方勢力一直以來都被認為是與資源浪費結合。 |

| | |
|---|---|
| **property casualty insurance**<br>產物災害保險 | Our firm offers **property casualty insurance** services particularly geared toward e-commerce.<br>我們公司提供產物災害保險，尤其針對電子商品。 |
| **pull (someone's) weight**<br>努力 | If he doesn't start **pulling** his **weight** around here, I am going to complain to our manager.<br>如果他再不用心點工作，我就要去報告我們的經理了。 |
| **pull the plug on**<br>抽離；解除 | Moira was devastated to learn the company was **pulling the plug on** several of her department's key projects.<br>當摩拉知道公司決定把她手上的一些重要案子抽走時，他感到很沮喪。 |

| | |
|---|---|
| **put a strain on**<br>造成負擔 | Paula's refusal to apologize for her comments **put a strain on** her relationship with her colleague.<br>寶拉不願意為她的評語道歉一事讓她和同事間的關係更顯緊張。 |
| **put it on plastic**<br>用信用卡 | If you haven't got enough cash, I'll **put it on plastic** and you can pay me back later.<br>如果你沒有足夠的現金，我可以先用信用卡幫你付，你之後再還給我。 |
| **put (something) on (somebody's) tab**<br>記在帳上 | Ken is paying for all the drinks tonight so just tell the barman to **put** everything **on** his **tab**.<br>肯會付今天晚上所有的酒錢，所以告訴酒保所有都記在他的帳上。 |

| | |
|---|---|
| **put together**<br>整合 | As part of his application to the art college, the student had to **put together** a portfolio of his work.<br>申請藝術學校的學生，必須將自己的作品集結成冊，成為申請表的一部分。 |
| **queue up**<br>排隊 | The rock group were so popular that fans would frequently **queue up** overnight to make sure they got tickets to their gigs.<br>這個搖滾樂團非常受歡迎，他們的歌迷會徹夜排隊確保可以買到演唱會的票 |
| **raining cats and dogs**<br>下大雨 | It looks like our plans to go camping this weekend will have to be put off for another day as the weather broadcast says it will be **raining cats and dogs**.<br>看來我們週末去露營的計畫要另外擇期了，因為氣象預報說會下大雨。 |

| | |
|---|---|
| **reach out to**<br>觸角伸到 | The local government's new social program was designed to **reach out to** disadvantaged youth.<br>當地政府新的社會政策，是設計來要將觸角延伸到較貧困的年輕人。 |
| **recipe for success [disaster]**<br>成功〔失敗〕的原因 | Putting Keith in charge of organizing our year-end party was a **recipe for disaster**.<br>讓契司來安排我們的尾牙是注定這次晚會辦得不好的主因。 |
| **red tape**<br>繁瑣的文件 | The customer service department has informed us that there is a lot of **red tape** to get through before we can even begin processing this inquiry.<br>客服部門通知我們在我們開始這個要求的程序前，有很多繁瑣的公文要處理。 |

| | |
|---|---|
| **resign to**<br>接受事實 | Malcolm had started to become **resigned to** the idea that he would never progress in the organization.<br>莫爾侃終於開始接受他在公司無法晉升的事實。 |
| **rock bottom**<br>最低潮 | Having lost her job and had her house repossessed, Margot had hit **rock bottom.**<br>丟了工作，房子又被銀行收回，瑪歌真是處在人生低潮。 |
| **roll out**<br>推出，上市 | Fast-fashion companies like Zara **roll out** products at break-neck speed these days.<br>快速時尚的公司，譬如Zara最近都是非常快速地推出新產品。 |

| | |
|---|---|
| **roughly speaking**<br>大致上而言 | Here on the graph we can see a spike of about 20 percent during the first quarter of the year, **roughly speaking**.<br>大體而言，我們在圖上可以看到在第一季，大約有百分之二十的獲利。 |
| **round up [down]**<br>加價〔減價〕 | If you put in an order for 450 units, we're prepared to **round** the number of units in your shipment **up** to 500.<br>如果你現在訂到450個單位，我們準備將你訂單貨物數量加量到500。 |
| **sales pitch**<br>推銷的說辭 | Adrian's **sales pitches** were so good that he could win over even the most difficult customers.<br>艾德里的推銷話術非常好，即使很難搞的客人都可以被他收服。 |

| | |
|---|---|
| **secure a loan**<br>取得貸款 | In order to **secure a loan** with this bank, you have to demonstrate a reasonable credit rating.<br>為了要得到銀行的貸款，你必須要提供一個合理的信用評等。 |
| **sell like hot cakes**<br>非常受歡迎 | As soon as the band releases a new album it starts **selling like hot cakes.**<br>這個樂團一發新專輯就大賣。 |
| **settle upon**<br>決定 | Have you **settled upon** a venue for the engagement party yet?<br>你決定你的訂婚宴的地點了嗎？ |

| | |
|---|---|
| **shake up**<br>振作 | Tech experts have agreed that the communications giant has **shaken up** the industry with its latest innovations.<br>科技專家都同意這位通信業的巨人用它的最新發明提振了產業。 |
| **shore up**<br>穩住 | Several attacks on the military camp convinced the commander of the need to **shore up** the defenses.<br>好幾次的軍營遭受攻擊讓指揮官相信有必要穩住他們的防守了。 |
| **simply put**<br>簡言之 | **Simply put**, our line of cosmetics offers better quality and value for money than any of our competitors.<br>簡言之，我們的化妝品，跟任何我們的競爭廠商相比，我們提供較好的品質和價值。 |

| | |
|---|---|
| **skid row**<br>貧民區 | Homeless and destitute, the tramp was living on **skid row**.<br>無家可歸又身無長物，這個流浪漢住在貧民窟裡。 |
| **slide (someone) into**<br>偷偷溜進 | Arriving late to class, Amanda quietly **slid** herself **into** a chair at the back of the room.<br>上課遲到了，阿曼達安靜的坐進教室後面的椅子裡。 |
| **slip under the radar**<br>不要被發現；維持低調 | As that clause in the agreement is disadvantageous to us, I presume it must have **slipped under the radar**.<br>條約中的那一個條文是不利於我們的，我想當初一定是沒有注意到。 |

**slug it out**
纏鬥

This month's inter-departmental meeting seemed to go on forever with the directors **slugging it out** over various issues.
這個月的部門會議由於經理們針對不同議題的反覆討論下，好像永遠開不完一樣。

**snatch up**
奪走

By the time I got to the bookstore, all the copies of the bestseller had already been **snatched up**.
當我到達書店時，那本暢銷書都已經被搶購一空了。

**soften the blow**
降低影響

Though the redundancy payout was sizable, it did not help **soften the blow** the employees felt.
雖然遣散費的金額不算小，但是並不會因此而讓員工感覺比較好。

| | |
|---|---|
| **(somebody) can't stress (something) enough** 不能再強調了〔十分重要〕 | I **can't stress** the importance of taking care of your health **enough**. 我真的無法再強調照顧好你的健康的重要性了。 |
| **(someone) get to hand it to (someone)** 放手 | You've **got to hand it to** Percy, he really does have a way with words. 你必須讓伯西接手，他真的對於文字比較在行。 |
| **(someone/something) carry a lot of weight** 十分重要 | Although she is rather quiet and unassuming, Hilda **carries a lot of weight** in this company. 雖然她很安靜又很謙虛，但是她可是公司的重要人物。 |

| | |
|---|---|
| **spar over**<br>爭執，意見不合 | The two colleagues verbally **sparred over** the most trivial incidents at almost every meeting.<br>那兩位同事在幾乎每場會議都會在雞毛蒜皮的小事上有口角。 |
| **spare no expense**<br>揮霍，無限度的花費 | Expect an extravagant affair for Celine's wedding reception as her father **spares no expense** on such occasions.<br>賽琳的父親在準備她的婚禮方面出手大方，所以可以預期她會有個豪華的婚禮。 |
| **spick and span**<br>清潔 | My desk is a complete disaster area, whereas my colleague keeps her work space **spick and span**.<br>我的桌子亂七八糟的，而我的同事的工作區總是清潔無比。 |

| | |
|---|---|
| **squeeze out**<br>剩出 | When the two companies merged, several employees had to be **squeezed out**.<br>當兩間公司合併時，部分員工必須要被犧牲。 |
| **stack up**<br>成為結果 | Going through the numbers for the third time, the accountant still could not see how they **stacked up**.<br>雖然算了第三次了，這位會計還是不清楚這些數字的來龍去脈。 |
| **stand above the rest**<br>領先群雄 | This painting **stands above the rest** as the finest example of post-impressionist art.<br>這幅畫在所有畫中脫穎而出，是後印象畫派裡的最佳例子。 |

| | |
|---|---|
| **stay put**<br>待在原處 | We can leave the dog here while we go and withdraw some cash from the ATM. He's very well-behaved and will always **stay put**.<br>我們可以把狗留在這裡，我們去提款機領錢。牠很乖不會亂跑。 |
| **stay the course**<br>堅持 | Most of my friends can **stay the course** when we go out all night, but Frank often has to leave early.<br>當我們出去玩整晚時，我們大部分朋友都可以全程一起玩，但是法蘭克通常都要先走。 |
| **stock up**<br>囤積 | Ahead of the typhoon, everyone was **stocking up** on the bare essentials.<br>在颱風前，大家都在囤積民生必需品。 |

| | |
|---|---|
| **stress (someone) out**<br>讓某人緊張 | The hustle bustle on the MRT into work every day really **stresses me out**.<br>每天在捷運上的匆忙和推擠真的讓我很緊張。 |
| **strike a balance**<br>設法達到平衡 | **Striking a balance** between price and quality has become a challenge for manufacturers of tablets who are trying to compete with the iPad.<br>嘗試要與iPad競爭的面版廠商都面臨了價格和品質的拉鋸難題。 |
| **strike up acquaintances**<br>建立友誼 | During my travels in Europe, I **struck up acquaintances** with many friendly people.<br>我在歐洲旅遊期間，和許多友善的人交了朋友。 |

| | |
|---|---|
| **subprime mortgage crisis**<br>次級房貸風暴 | Economists are split over what role the **subprime mortgage crisis** played in the financial meltdown.<br>經濟學家對次級房貸風暴在此次金融危機中扮演的角色有不同的看法。 |
| **suit (someone's) fancy**<br>合（某人）口味 | That new handbag I saw in the store window yesterday would really **suit** my wife's **fancy**.<br>我昨天在櫥窗理看見的那個包包一定會合我老婆的口味。 |
| **surefire**<br>不二法門 | Exercise and a healthy diet are **surefire** methods of losing weight.<br>運動和健康的飲食是減肥的不二法門。 |

| | |
|---|---|
| **take a lot of blows**<br>受創多次 | Despite **taking a lot of blows** in the press recently, the president still has a high popularity rating.<br>即使最近在媒體上有多次受創負面形象，總統仍然有很高的人氣。 |
| **take decisive action on**<br>採取具決斷力的行動 | Unless we **take decisive action on** this soon, the problem could spiral out of control.<br>除非我們立即採取行動，這個問題有可能會失控。 |
| **take measures**<br>採取措施 | The country is **taking measures** to ensure we are protected from the flooding that affected us in previous years.<br>這個國家正在採取措施確保我們可以不受前幾年那場水災的影響。 |

| | |
|---|---|
| **take the blame**<br>承擔指責 | You'll just have to **take the blame** and get on with things for it was you who caused this mess.<br>你必須承擔這個指責並讓事情繼續，因為是你把事情弄糟的。 |
| **take the helm**<br>接班；主導 | Since **taking the helm**, the new CEO has implemented a radical shakeup to the way we operate.<br>自從我們新的執行長接手公司以來，他對我們運作方式實施了一個很大的改變。 |
| **talk (some-one) into (some-thing)**<br>說服某人做某事 | Let's try to **talk** Dolores **into** com-ing on the skiing trip with us next month.<br>讓我們一起來試著說服多羅爾下個月跟我們一起去滑雪之旅。 |

| | |
|---|---|
| **tap for**<br>指定 | Ralph has done so well since joining our team that he is already being **tapped for** a management role.<br>羅夫自從加入我們的團隊後表現極佳，所以他已經被內定為經理級的人選了。 |
| **tap into**<br>接通 | To increase its influence abroad, the sports brand is attempting to **tap into** emerging markets.<br>要提升這個運動品牌的海外影響力，它們打算前進新興市場。 |
| **teeter on the edge [brink]**<br>在邊緣遊走 | Despite **teetering on the edge** of financial collapse, the bank managed to stay afloat with the aid of a government bailout package.<br>雖然這間銀行已經面臨倒閉的危機，在政府的紓困案的幫助下，他們設法維持營運。 |

| | |
|---|---|
| **that's it**<br>就這樣吧！ | OK, **that's it** for today, everyone. Thanks for attending.<br>好的，今天就到這裡了。謝謝大家的參加。 |
| **the floor**<br>主控權 | And now, I'd like to give **the floor** to our CEO, Mr. David Brent.<br>現在，我把時間交給我們的執行長，大衛布藍特先生。 |
| **the here and now**<br>眼前 | There's no point in discussing our long-term targets when what we really need is to address our goals in **the here and now**.<br>討論我們的長期目標似乎不是當務之急，我們應該著眼在目前的目標。 |

| | |
|---|---|
| **the ins and outs**<br>詳細情形 | During my first week, I had trouble understanding **the ins and outs** of my new job, but with the help of my colleagues I was soon up to speed.<br>我剛開始新工作的第一週，我對工作內容的瞭解感到很困難，可是在同事的幫助下，我很快就上了軌道。 |
| **the picture of (something)**<br>現象，狀況 | Now that Josh has settled down with his fiancée and a steady job, he seems **the picture of** happiness.<br>現在賈許有了穩定的工作和未婚妻，他看起來十分快樂。 |
| **there's a catch**<br>條件；要求 | As with all these free offers that you find online, I think **there's a catch**.<br>你在網路上找到的這些免費的好康，我覺得箇中必有蹊蹺。 |

| | |
|---|---|
| **thick skin**<br>厚臉皮 | With all the criticism you have to face, you need a really **thick skin** to survive in this industry.<br>有這麼多你需要面對的批評，你真的需要很厚臉皮才能在這個產業繼續生存哦！ |
| **throw in the towel**<br>認輸；放棄 | Sometimes when things are going wrong, I feel like just **throwing in the towel** and starting all over again.<br>有時候當事情不對勁時，我會覺得就認輸，從頭來過。 |
| **tickle pink**<br>逗得開心 | Thank you so much for your gift; it really **tickled** me **pink**.<br>謝謝你的禮物，收到它真的讓我很開心。 |

| | |
|---|---|
| **tighten (some-body's) belt**<br>減少（某人的）開支 | If we're going to stand any chance of saving for that vacation in summer, we will definitely have to **tighten** our **belts**.<br>如果我們要為了夏天的度假把握任何機會省錢，我們真的要認真減少開支。 |
| **to be a shambles**<br>混亂，不穩 | Because she has been so reckless with her spending, Tina's finances **are** now **a shambles**.<br>由於提娜花錢時太過衝動，她目前的財務狀況十分不穩健。 |
| **tough luck**<br>不走運 | **Tough luck** failing your driving test, but I'm sure you'll ace it next time.<br>我覺得你這次沒通過駕照考試是運氣不好，下次一定可以通過的。 |

| | |
|---|---|
| **under wraps**<br>保密；封鎖 | If I tell you something, you have to promise to keep it **under wraps**.<br>如果我跟你說，你要承諾一定保密。 |
| **up (some-one's) sleeve**<br>（某人在）打什麼主意 | How can we give Holly a big surprise for her birthday? Have you got any-thing **up** your **sleeve**?<br>我們要如何給荷莉一個大大的生日驚喜呢？ 你有什麼想法嗎？ |
| **up the ante**<br>有助益 | In order to match its competitors this year, the supermarket chain will have to **up the ante** in terms of improving its range of products.<br>為了在今年裡與競爭者抗衡，這間連鎖超級市場將加強它的產品品項來提升助益。 |

| | |
|---|---|
| **up the creek without a paddle**<br>糟糕了 | When Ursula didn't show up for the presentation, she really left me **up the creek without a paddle**.<br>當烏蘇拉沒有出席報告，她真的讓我身陷麻煩了。 |
| **up to (some-body's) ears in (some-thing)**<br>（某人的）工作十分繁重 | My accountant won't be able to go through the tax return with me until Thursday as she is **up to** her **ears in** paperwork.<br>我的會計師要到下週四才能幫我處理退稅，因為她目前的工作太多了。 |
| **uphill battle**<br>情勢艱難 | Ahead of the tournament, the tennis player faced an **uphill battle** to get fit.<br>在這個比賽之前，這位網球選手正在非常辛苦地減肥。 |

| | |
|---|---|
| **venture capital**<br>風險投資 | For any new business to have a chance of success, a decent amount of **venture capital** is required.<br>任何生意要有成功的機會，一個起碼的風險資本是一定要的。 |
| **walk in the park**<br>容易的事 | While some of her classmates struggled, Iris found her history exam a complete **walk in the park**.<br>當愛麗斯的同學都為了歷史考試痛苦時，她反而覺得十分容易。 |
| **weather the storm**<br>通過考驗 | The firm's success is proof that they have finally managed to **weather the storm**.<br>這間公司的成功證明他們終究設法度過了考驗。 |

| | |
|---|---|
| **weigh down**<br>頹喪，低迷 | As talented as he was, for many years the young violinist felt **weighed down** by his family's expectations.<br>雖然很有才華，但是這位年輕的小提琴家在家人多年來對他的期許下一直感到很頹喪。 |
| **wild guess**<br>隨便猜 | At a **wild guess**, I'd say there were about 10,000 people at the festival.<br>我隨便猜猜，這個盛會應該有一萬人參加吧！ |
| **withstand wear and tear**<br>禁得起考驗 | These hiking boots have **withstood** years of **wear and tear** and are still in relatively good condition.<br>這雙登山鞋真的是耐穿，而且看起來還是蠻好的。 |

| | |
|---|---|
| **work out**<br>健身；解決 | Despite **working out** for several hours every week, Gerard could never put on any muscle.<br>儘管一週健身好幾個小時，捷若德還是沒有任何肌肉。<br>Did you **work out** your problems with your girlfriend yet?<br>你解決了跟你女朋友之間的問題了嗎？ |
| **work the room**<br>與人們交際應酬 | Eliza is really shy and has no idea how to **work the room** at business functions.<br>伊莱莎很害羞，而且在生意場合總是不知該如何與人交際應酬。 |

Note

Note

國家圖書館出版品預行編目資料

1日1分鐘新多益必考單字片語背誦集／劉慧如, James Baron 編著. ——初版. ——臺北市：書泉，2014.12

面；　公分

ISBN 978-986-121-972-1（平裝附光碟片）

1. 多益測驗　2.詞彙　3.慣用語

805. 1895　　103020497

3AN0

# 1日1分鐘新多益必考單字片語背誦集

編 著 者　劉慧如（370.1）、James Baron
發 行 人　楊榮川
總 編 輯　王翠華
責任編輯　陳秀菁
版型設計　吳佳臻
封面設計　吳佳臻

出 版 者　書泉出版社
地　　址：台北市大安區106
和平東路二段339號4樓
電　　話：(02)2705-5066（代表號）
傳　　真：(02)2706-6100
網　　址：http://www.wunan.com.tw
電子郵件：shuchuan@shuchuan.com.tw
劃撥帳號：01303853
戶　　名：書泉出版社

經 銷 商　朝日文化
進退貨地址：新北市中和區橋安街15巷1號7樓
TEL：(02)2249-7714　　FAX：(02)2249-8715

法律顧問　林勝安律師事務所　林勝安律師

版　　刷　2012年7月　初版一刷
2014年12月　二版一刷

定　　價　150元整

初版由文字復興出版。